Franklin's Bad Day

Franklin

Franklin is a trademark of Kids Can Press Ltd.

Text © 1996 Contextx Inc.
Illustrations © 1996 Brenda Clark Illustrator Inc.
Interior illustrations prepared with the assistance of
Muriel Hughes Wood.

Published in Canada and the U.S. by Kids Can Press Ltd.
25 Dockside Drive, Toronto, ON M5A 0B5

Kids Can Press is a Corus Entertainment Inc. company

www.kidscanpress.com

Printed and bound Buji, Shenzhen, China, in 1/2021 by WKT Company

CM 96 0 9 8 7 6 5 4
CDN PA 96 / CMC PA 15 0 9 8 7 6 5

Library and Archives Canada Cataloguing in Publication

Bourgeois, Paulette
     Franklin's bad day / written by Paulette Bourgeois ; Brenda Clark
[illustrations].

ISBN 978-1-55453-732-7

1. Franklin (Fictitious character : Bourgeois) — Juvenile fiction. I. Clark,
Brenda II. Title.

PS8553.O85477F836

Kids Can Press gratefully acknowledges that the land on which our
office is located is the traditional territory of many nations, including
the Mississaugas of the Credit, the Anishnabeg, the Chippewa, the
Haudenosaunee and the Wendat peoples, and is now home to many
diverse First Nations, Inuit and Métis peoples.

We thank the Government of Ontario, through Ontario Creates;
the Ontario Arts Council; the Canada Council for the Arts; and the
Government of Canada for supporting our publishing activity.

Franklin's Bad Day

Written by Paulette Bourgeois
Illustrated by Brenda Clark

Kids Can Press

FRANKLIN loved to play outside in winter. He
could skate forwards and backwards. He liked to
catch snowflakes on his tongue and make angels
in the snow. But today was different. Franklin was
having a very bad day.

It started in the morning. Franklin was grumpy when he woke up.

"That's a grouchy face," teased his father.

"Yes, it is," said Franklin. He crossed his arms and frowned.

"Would you like a nice breakfast?" asked his mother.

"No!" said Franklin.

His mother made breakfast anyway.

Franklin stared out the window. Heavy gray clouds pushed across the sky.

"It's even a bad day outside," grumbled Franklin.

He picked at his food.

For the rest of the morning, nothing went right.

Franklin knocked over his juice and broke his favorite cup. He couldn't find his marbles, and the last piece of his puzzle was missing.

Franklin slammed a door and stomped his feet.

"You seem awfully cranky," said his mother.

"I am not!" shouted Franklin.

Just then, Bear knocked on the door. Franklin
peeked out.

"Do you want to make a snowman or ride on
my sled?" asked Bear.

Franklin sighed. "I don't want to do *anything*."

"Please?" Bear said.

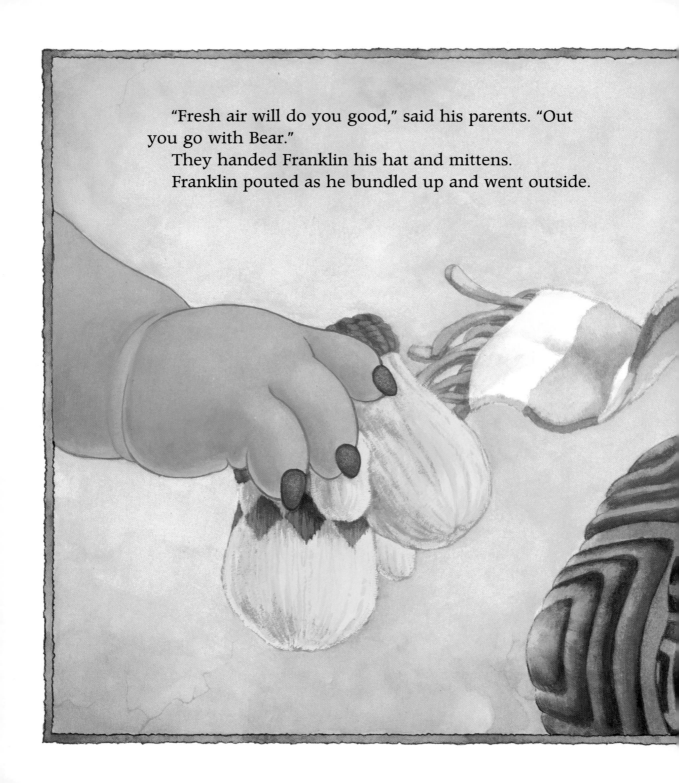

"Fresh air will do you good," said his parents. "Out you go with Bear."

They handed Franklin his hat and mittens.

Franklin pouted as he bundled up and went outside.

The two friends walked along the path near Otter's house.

"Let's ask Otter to come," said Bear.

Franklin gave Bear a puzzled look.

"Oh, I forgot," said Bear sadly. "Otter moved away yesterday."

They didn't talk all the way to the hill.

Franklin kneeled at the front of the sled and
Bear sat behind him.

Bear gave a push. "Let's go!" he shouted.

The sled glided halfway down the slope. And
then it stopped. They had landed on a bare patch.

"Oh, no!" wailed Franklin. "What a terrible day!"

The hill was no fun, so Beaver suggested they go to the pond.

When they arrived, the pond was roped off.

"No skating today," warned Mr. Mole. "The ice is thin."

Franklin lost his temper. "This is my worstest day ever!"

"There's no such word as worstest," said Beaver.

"There is for me!" said Franklin. "I'm leaving!"

Franklin stormed home.

He threw his skates and his slushy, mushy mittens on the floor.

"Please pick up your things," said his mother.

"NO!" he yelled.

Franklin was sent to his room.

Franklin was so furious that he kicked
his castle.

His father came running when he heard the
crash. "What's going on here?"

Franklin lay on the floor and cried.

"Don't worry," said his father. "You can build
the castle again."

"But I made that castle with Otter, and she's
not here anymore," sobbed Franklin.

"Oh, now I understand," said Franklin's father. "You're mad and sad because your friend moved away."

Franklin nodded.

"And you miss her a lot," his father said.

"Yes," agreed Franklin in a small voice.

They hugged each other for a long time.

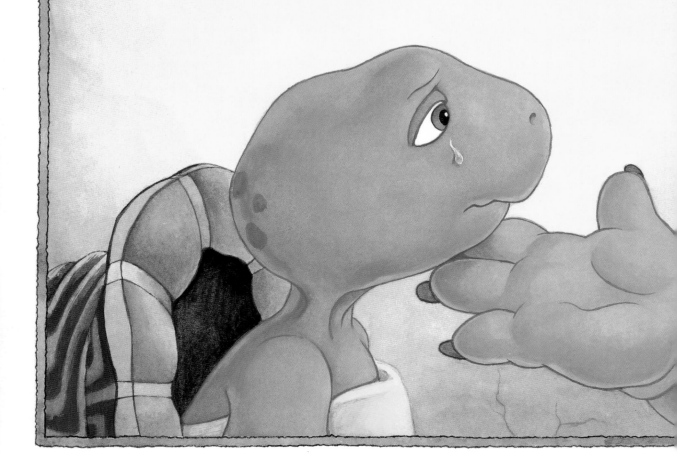

"Otter and I did lots of things together," said Franklin. "Now we can't."

"You can still be friends," said Franklin's father. "You can share your feelings by calling or writing."

Franklin thought for a moment.

"Do we have a big envelope and some stamps?" he asked.

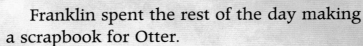

Franklin spent the rest of the day making
a scrapbook for Otter.

He filled it with pictures and drawings of the
two friends together.

Near the back, Franklin put a dozen
envelopes. He printed his address on each one.

On the last page, he wrote:

> *Please write to me. Then we can*
> *stay friends forever.*

As he walked to the mailbox, Franklin felt better.
Snow was falling and it was getting cold enough
for the pond to freeze.

Franklin had a feeling that tomorrow would be a
good day.